Sometimes When I'm Mad

Deborah Serani, Psy.D.
illustrated by Kyra Teis

free spirit
PUBLISHING®

Library of Congress Cataloging-in-Publication Data
Names: Serani, Deborah, 1961– author. | Teis, Kyra, illustrator.
Title: Sometimes when I'm mad / by Deborah Serani, Psy.D. ; illustrated by Kyra Teis.
Other titles: Sometimes when I am mad
Description: Minneapolis : Free Spirit Publishing Inc., 2021. | Audience: Ages 4–8
Identifiers: LCCN 2020050634 (print) | LCCN 2020050635 (ebook) | ISBN 9781631986093 (hardcover) |
    ISBN 9781631986109 (pdf) | ISBN 9781631986116 (epub)
Subjects: LCSH: Anger—Juvenile literature. | Emotions—Juvenile literature. | Child psychology—Juvenile literature.
Classification: LCC BF723.A4 S427 2021 (print) | LCC BF723.A4 (ebook) | DDC 155.4/1247—dc23
LC record available at https://lccn.loc.gov/2020050634
LC ebook record available at https://lccn.loc.gov/2020050635

Free Spirit Publishing does not have control over or assume responsibility for author or third-party websites and their content.

Reading Level Grade 1; Interest Level Ages 4–8;
Fountas & Pinnell Guided Reading Level I

Edited by Alison Behnke
Cover and interior design by Emily Dyer

10 9 8 7 6 5 4 3 2 1
Printed in China
R18860521

Free Spirit Publishing Inc.
6325 Sandburg Road, Suite 100
Minneapolis, MN 55427-3674
(612) 338-2068
help4kids@freespirit.com
freespirit.com

FSC
www.fsc.org
MIX
Paper from
responsible sources
FSC® C144853

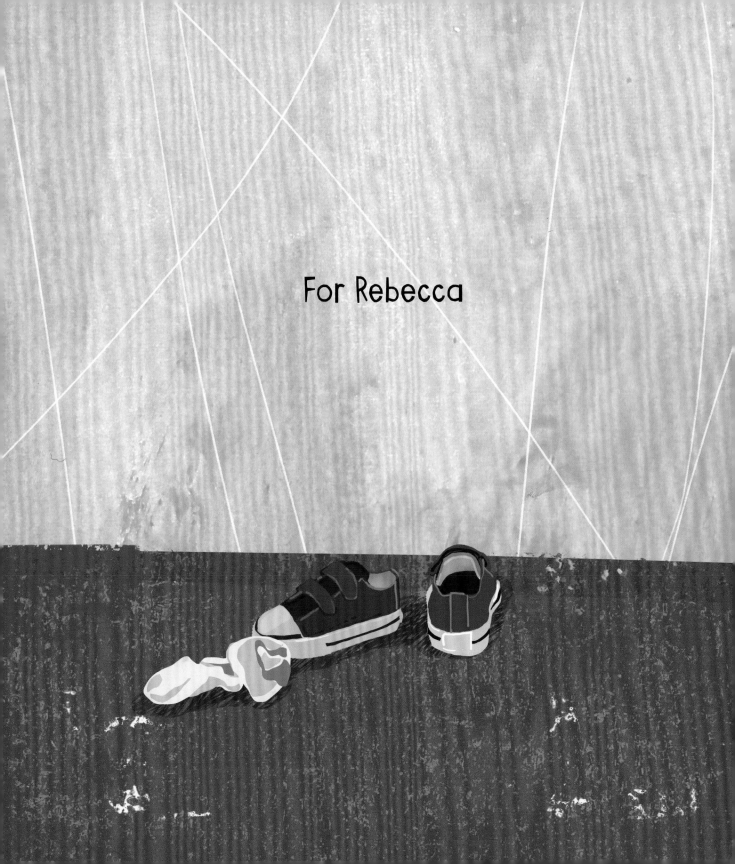

For Rebecca

Sometimes when I'm mad, it's because everything goes wrong.

I spill my milk.

I can't find my favorite toy.

My friend doesn't come over to play.

Mama says we all get mad. Sometimes when we're mad, it's because we can't control what's happening.

She says I can focus on what I can control. When my friend doesn't come over, Mama names two things I could do instead and asks me to pick one. "Do you want to do a puzzle or play a game?"

I say, "Let's do the puzzle."

And I feel better.

Sometimes when I'm mad,
nothing feels right.

My socks are too scratchy.

My oatmeal's too lumpy.

Or my bath water is too cold.

Papa says sometimes when we feel mad,
we may be tired. Everything bothers us.

He asks if I want to rest on the couch, read a book together, or take a nap in my bed.

I say, "I'll rest on the couch."

And I feel better.

Sometimes when I'm mad,
my body doesn't feel good.

My tummy aches, or my heart
thumps, or my head feels heavy.

Grandma says sometimes when we're mad, our body can feel achy or shaky.

She tells me I can ask for a hug or a cool washcloth for my head. Or I can ask her to rub my back or tummy.

I say, "I'd like a hug."

And I feel better.

Sometimes when I'm mad, I do things that don't help at all.

I don't listen to Papa.

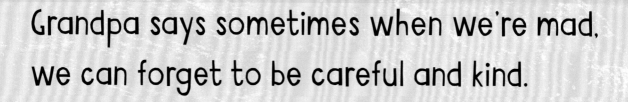

Grandpa says sometimes when we're mad,
we can forget to be careful and kind.

He tells me I can take a
deep breath, say I'm sorry,
or try to make things right.

I say, "I'll go and make things right."

And I feel better.

Sometimes when I'm mad, my feelings are icky and tricky.

I don't know what to say or how to act.

My teacher says sometimes when we're mad, it's hard to understand exactly what we're feeling and why.

He tells me I can talk about my feelings with Mama or Papa or someone else I love.

I can talk to a good friend.

Or I can talk to him.

I say, "I'll talk with Mama."

And I feel better.

HELPING CHILDREN THROUGH ANGER
A Guide for Caring Adults

Anger is an intense emotion. It is a natural response to certain issues or situations, yet is often felt or expressed in ways that are scary, confusing, or even unhealthy. Many people consider anger a "bad" emotion and view its expression as destructive. As a result, experiencing anger can be difficult for both children and adults. Indeed, anger is a feeling most people prefer *not* to experience. But when we understand anger, it can become a healing, transformative, and empowering force.

Most children require guidance, support, and instruction as they learn to identify and regulate angry emotions. It's not always easy for little ones to understand feeling mad. Among children, difficulties with anger are linked to physical experiences like headaches, stomach pains, increased heart rate and blood pressure, and appetite and sleeping problems. *Maladaptive* anger—anger that is unmanaged or highly aggressive—is also linked to academic difficulties, social and emotional delays, anxiety, depression, conduct disorders, and family stress. However, when children are able to express anger in *adaptive* ways, they can find solutions to problems, create structure and healthy rules for themselves and others, build self-confidence, and experience greater physical and emotional well-being.

While we want children to be able to express their anger, we also want to help them release these feelings in constructive ways. It's equally important to show children how to repair social connections and self-esteem when angry feelings come out in muddled or messy ways. *Sometimes When I'm Mad* helps children understand how anger feels, what it looks like, how to cope with it, and how unresolved experiences can trigger it. By reading this book, you'll help little ones learn to identify their feelings. Children will also be better able to notice when factors like hunger, fatigue, or disappointment are contributing to angry feelings.

HOW TO SPOT ANGER IN CHILDREN OF VARIOUS AGES

Anger looks different in children of varying ages. And of course, every child is unique in personality and expression. However, children do tend to demonstrate certain patterns at different developmental stages. Knowing these patterns can help you better understand and support the children you care for.

Infants: While newborns may express irritability and frustration, these expressions are generally not emotionally triggered, but rather needs-based. Feeling cold, hungry, wet, frightened, or tired will set into motion an irritable cry response from a baby. As newborns age, they become more socially and emotionally aware of their world. Babies begin to truly express anger at about six months. They may respond angrily with fussing, biting, and crying directed toward things or people who thwart their goals or fail to meet undetected needs—from dropping a toy or bottle to feeling discomfort.

Toddlers: Since toddlers often don't have the language to express what they're feeling, they typically express anger physically. It's common for them to display a variety of aggressive behaviors when they're mad, including crying, stomping, hitting, pushing, or breaking things. Toddlers frequently tantrum, having an average of nine tantrums a week. As toddlers gain more language and body control, they can learn to express their anger in more adaptive ways. But in general, this age group tends to struggle with angry feelings and behaviors.

Preschool-age children: Preschoolers typically interact more with peers than toddlers do, moving from independent play to socialized play. As preschoolers are still acquiring language skills and not always able to manage emotions, they can be easily frustrated when asked to share, take turns, or make transitions. They then express this frustration and anger in outward ways. Preschoolers often display anger in tantrums, meltdowns, and physical aggression like hitting, throwing, and even biting. Preschoolers may also experience aches and pains and other physical irritability as part of anger.

School-age children: Like younger children, school-age children often display anger through hitting, throwing, or breaking things. In fact, physical expressions of anger typically peak during this time. But as children develop greater language skills, they may also use verbally aggressive words and phrases to express anger. At the same time, as children get older and grow in emotional awareness, they learn how to regulate their emotions. They also become more reflective about angry emotions. They *feel* angry first, then *act*. Some children manage angry feelings successfully, while others may need additional guidance.

WAYS TO ENCOURAGE HEALTHY ANGER EXPRESSION

Helping children understand their own unique responses to anger—as well as *why* they are feeling angry—builds their social and emotional skills and resilience. They can then respond to their anger prosocially. Here are some ways adults can encourage healthy anger expression.

- Help children understand that anger is natural, everyone feels it, and it will pass. Acknowledge that feeling angry can be uncomfortable.

- Treat children's feelings—even ones that are inappropriately expressed—with respect.

- Help children learn positive and productive ways to express anger. Show them how to shake off irritability by doing jumping jacks or bouncing a ball outside. Teach little ones that saying "I'm mad" can communicate to others how they feel and also create space for talking more about it. For older children, activities like taking a walk, playing sports, or journaling can help. Encourage children to express anger in these appropriate ways, and model such behaviors for them.

- Identify ways anger may be inappropriately expressed, such as hitting, punching, throwing or breaking things, spitting, pulling hair, or biting. It's also important to address verbal expressions of anger. Teach children that yelling, name calling, bullying, and cursing are not acceptable ways to show anger. When presenting these ideas, it's vital to teach little ones that anger is natural and we aren't asking them to hold it in or ignore it. Instead, we want to help them express it in healthy ways.

- Create and communicate age-appropriate consequences for aggression or tantrums, such as calm-down zones or times for toddlers, preschoolers, and school-age children. A good guideline is that calm-down times for misbehavior should last one minute for each birthday (so, no time-outs for babies!). Another approach is to create if/then scenarios with positive reinforcement when you see a child's anger escalating. For example, "If you count to five and calm down, then we can go outside to play." Or, "If you squeeze your stress ball, then you'll start to feel better."

- Encourage open and honest communication about anger and other feelings. Many situations may spark anger in children, such as feeling powerless or misunderstood, struggling with poor self-esteem, being unable to understand or keep up with schoolwork, having few or no friends, or being teased or bullied. When children share these experiences, adults can help them handle issues effectively, including addressing sources of anger and managing angry feelings before they get out of control.

- Help children learn how to ask adults for help coping with anger. It can be a challenge to get little ones to open up about difficulties, because children often worry that if they share problems with parents or other caring adults, the adults will be worried or upset. Use direct statements and open-ended questions. "You can talk to me about anything" or "I'm here for you no matter what" are trust-building sayings that help children feel safe and loved. Avoid yes-or-no questions. "Tell me about school today" invites more conversation than "Did you have a good day?" Focus on children's positive behaviors and actions. "Tell me how you used your words today during recess," or "What did you say to your brother when he hurt your feelings?" Helping children identify their successful actions will build self-esteem. When encouraging children to seek guidance or comfort regarding anger, use inviting questions like "How can I help you feel better?" With older children, consider creating structured times to check in. Make it a point to talk each day about what's on children's minds and how they're feeling. These moments will lay the foundations for a lifetime of healthy connection and communication.

- Help children identify how anger feels in their bodies. Anger is complex, often surging neurochemically before we're consciously aware of it. Teaching children to detect anger will help them manage it. Let them know anger can make them feel hot, sweaty, and uncomfortable, or leave them feeling cold, afraid, and worried. Their heart may thump, their tummy could ache, or their head might hurt. They might purse their lips, frown, or cry. They might stand stiffly or stomp around. You could model an angry face or body language so children can recognize it, or ask children to draw what angry and calm faces look like. The more you talk about how anger can feel, the less scary it becomes. In addition, it lowers the chances that little ones will suppress or ignore their anger.

- Teach children ways to calm and soothe themselves, including taking a deep breath and counting aloud to five, cuddling a comforting object like a blanket or a stuffed animal, taking a rest in a quiet room, reading a book, coloring, or listening to music.

WHEN SPECIAL NEEDS REQUIRE SPECIAL INTERVENTIONS

If a child demonstrates patterns of irritability over a long course of time, other issues such as the following may be influencing their anger.

- *Attention deficit hyperactivity disorder (ADHD):* Children who experience ADHD are easily frustrated and often act impulsively. Children with ADHD tend to be more physically than verbally expressive and may require more intensive interventions to reduce aggression, anger, and irritability.

- *Autism spectrum disorder (ASD):* Children on the autism spectrum typically experience difficulty regulating emotional responses. They can often feel anxious and agitated when overwhelmed. Furthermore, unexpected changes in routine can cause frustration and feelings of helplessness, which are often expressed in physical ways. Children with autism will need special attention and support to help them cope with anger.

- *Sensory processing disorders:* Children who encounter difficulties understanding the information they receive from their body may have sensory processing disorders. Experiences like too much noise or light, scratchy clothes, or being around large groups of people can overwhelm and frustrate children with these difficulties, leading to anger and aggression. Unique interventions and self-soothing tools will be needed at home and school.

- *Undiagnosed learning disability:* If a child demonstrates anger, expresses extreme frustration, or lashes out verbally or physically while doing schoolwork, this may be a result of an undiagnosed learning disability. Assessment of a child's intellectual ability will identify weaknesses as well as strengths. This knowledge can then be used to bolster academic confidence and emotional expression.

WHEN TO SEEK PROFESSIONAL HELP

Understanding more about how children may show anger at different ages or due to various needs will help you support them as they learn to express these feelings in healthy ways. Keep in mind that replacing inappropriate behaviors with more appropriate ones will be relatively easy in some situations and harder in others. It's important to give children time to learn new behaviors and to expect the journey to be filled with gains, slips, and some sidesteps. Be consistent and supportive, and try to always model healthy expressions of anger yourself. If you do demonstrate anger in an unhealthy way, know that it can be powerful if you talk about your misstep and propose a better way to handle the situation the next time.

If these tips and techniques fail to help, and a child's anger becomes more frequent and intense, it may be time to seek help from a mental health professional. Consultation with a specialist can determine if anger-related disorders, sometimes called *externalizing disorders*, may be occurring. Proper treatment can help children, families, and educators find relief.

RESOURCES FOR MORE INFORMATION AND SUPPORT

Association for Children's Mental Health acmh-mi.org

Autistic Self Advocacy Network (ASAN) autisticadvocacy.org

Child Mind Institute childmind.org

Children and Adults with Attention Deficit/Hyperactivity Disorder chadd.org

Learning Disabilities Association of America ldaamerica.org

Mindful Schools mindfulschools.org

National Anger Management Association namass.org

National Education Association nea.org

National Foster Parent Association nfpaonline.org

National Institute of Mental Health nimh.nih.gov

National Parenting Education Network npen.org

National PTA pta.org

STAR Institute for Sensory Processing Disorder spdstar.org

Zero to Three zerotothree.org

ABOUT THE AUTHOR AND ILLUSTRATOR OF THE SOMETIMES WHEN COLLECTION

Deborah Serani, Psy.D., is an award-winning author and psychologist who has been in practice for thirty years. She is also a professor at Adelphi University. Dr. Serani is a go-to expert for psychological issues. Her writing on depression and trauma has been published in many academic journals, and her interviews can be found in *Newsday*, *Psychology Today*, *The Chicago Tribune*, *The New York Times*, *The Associated Press*, and affiliate radio programs at CBS and NPR, among others. She is also a TEDx speaker. Dr. Serani lives on Long Island, New York.

Kyra Teis is a children's book author-illustrator, a graphic novelist, and an avid sewer of costumes and clothing. She works in a cozy studio in central New York, which is crammed full of books and fabrics from all over the world. When she's not making art, you can find her and her husband cheering wildly at their two daughters' soccer games and musical theater productions.

Other Great Books from Free Spirit

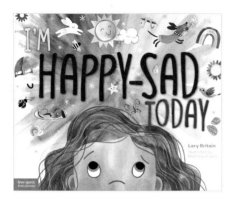

I'm Happy-Sad Today
Making Sense of Mixed-Together Feelings
by Lory Britain, Ph.D., illustrated by Matthew Rivera
For ages 3–8. 40 pp.; HC; full-color; 11¼" x 9¼".

Cool Down and Work Through Anger
by Cheri J. Meiners, M.Ed.
For ages 4–8. 40 pp.; PB; full-color; 9" x 9"; includes digital content.

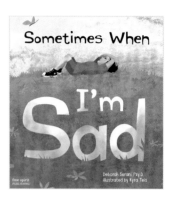

Sometimes When I'm Sad
by Deborah Serani, Psy.D., illustrated by Kyra Teis
For ages 4-8. 40 pp.; HC; full-color; 8¼" x 9".

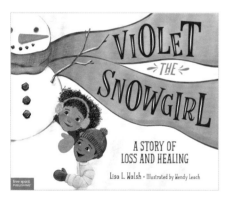

Violet the Snowgirl
A Story of Loss and Healing
by Lisa L. Walsh, illustrated by Wendy Leach
For ages 5–10. 36 pp.; HC; full-color; 11¼" x 9¼".

Put Your Worries Away
Kids Can Cope Series
by Gill Hasson, illustrated by Sarah Jennings
For ages 6–9. 32 pp.; HC; full-color; 10½" x 8¼".

Feeling Angry!
by Katie Douglass, illustrated by Mike Gordon
For ages 5–9. 32 pp.; HC; full-color; 7½" x 8¼".

Free Leader's Guide
freespirit.com/leader

Interested in purchasing multiple quantities and receiving volume discounts?
Contact edsales@freespirit.com or call 1.800.735.7323 and ask for Education Sales.

Many Free Spirit authors are available for speaking engagements, workshops, and keynotes.
Contact speakers@freespirit.com or call 1.800.735.7323.

For pricing information, to place an order, or to request a free catalog, contact:

Free Spirit Publishing Inc. • 6325 Sandburg Road • Suite 100 • Minneapolis, MN 55427-3674
toll-free 800.735.7323 • local 612.338.2068 • fax 612.337.5050 • help4kids@freespirit.com • freespirit.com